For Willa

Ballerina Flying

Copyright © 2002 by Alexa D. Brandenberg

Printed in Hong Kong. All rights reserved.

www.harperchildrens.com

Library of Congress Cataloging-in-Publication Data

Brandenberg, Alexa.

Ballerina flying / by Alexa Brandenberg.

p.   cm.

Summary: Mina, who loves dance and especially ballet,
is off to her Tuesday afternoon class with Miss Viola.

ISBN 0-06-029549-X — ISBN 0-06-029550-3 (lib. bdg.)

[1. Ballet dancing—Fiction.]   I. Title.

PZ7.B73625 Bal   2002   00-056721   [E]—dc21   CIP   AC

Typography by Stephanie Bart-Horvath

1 2 3 4 5 6 7 8 9 10

❖

First Edition

Ballerina Flying

Alexa Brandenberg

HarperCollins*Publishers*

My name is Mina and
I love to dance.

I like jazz dance, tap dance,

square dance, and ballroom dance.

But I like ballet dance best of all.

To me, ballet dance is like flying.

Every Tuesday afternoon
I go to ballet class.
Tuesday is my favorite day.

As soon as I get home
from school,
I put on my tutu.

I dance and dance around my room.

I dream of flying like a ballerina.

Before I know it, Dad
says it's time for ballet class.
Quickly I take off my tutu.
My teacher, Miss Viola, says
tutus are just for special
days, like recitals.
I can't wait for the
special days!

I tie up my hair.
Dad helps me.

I put on my tights,
my leotard,
and my soft leather shoes
with a strap to keep
them on.

My feet aren't strong enough yet, but
one day I will wear the satiny toe shoes
that the older girls wear.

Dad takes me to ballet school early. He knows I like to watch the older girls and boys dance. They look like they are flying.

But I know it's not as easy as it looks. Ballet takes a lot of practice and hard work.

I am ready to work hard. I want to fly, too.

In our classroom,
Miss Viola is happy to
see us.
We are happy to see
her, too.

Finally it's time to
dance!
Back straight, stomach in.

Ready?

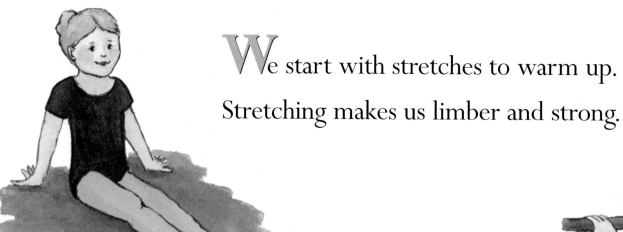

W e start with stretches to warm up.

Stretching makes us limber and strong.

Point your toes.

Flex your toes.

Bend forward.

Bend back.

Stretch sideways.

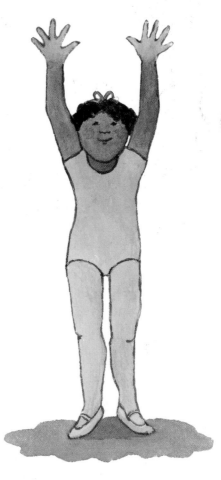

Reach way up high.

Next, we demonstrate the five positions. These are the most important positions in ballet because they are used in all the other steps.

The other steps have French names. I like the way they sound, but they are hard to pronounce. Miss Viola reminds us how to do and say the steps. We practice them over and over again.

1st position

2nd position

3rd position   4th position   5th position

We do our first exercises at the barre.

(That is "bar" in French!)

Plié *(plee-AY)*

Bend your knees.

Tendu *(tahn-DEW)*

Point your leg.

Grand Battement *(GRAHN baht-MAHN)*

Lift your leg high.

Then Miss Viola calls us out to the middle of the room, where we do the rest of our steps.

(That's Mr. Slotky at the piano!)

Relevé *(rel-VAY)*

Up on your toes.

Arabesque *(a-rah-BESK)*

Leg up, arms stretched

Pirouette *(peer-WET)*

Spin on one leg.

Jeté *(zhuh-TAY)*

Leap! Every week we leap a little higher.

When class is over, we bow to Miss Viola.

Révérence *(rev-RAHNS)*

Bow. I imagine I am wearing my tutu and bowing to a real audience.

I am one step closer to flying.